The Dog Man of Denny-Blaine

Paul Lonardo

Publisher's Note:

This is a work of fiction. All names, characters, places, and events are the work of the author's imagination.

Any resemblance to real persons, places, or events is coincidental.

Solstice Publishing -
http://www.solsticeempire.com/

Chapter One

The drive south from east central Seattle was not long enough to give Sandi time to reconsider what he had planned. He was never one to act recklessly, but this was different. Despite the inherent dangers of the undertaking, he had his mind made up. And when Sandoval Rivera Garcia Diaz decided to do something, it was as good as done. He simply was not going to play host to an animal that did not respect the boundaries in the human-dog relationship.

Doreen had been feeding the animal all winter, leaving leftover food outside by the edge of the woods. This was a kind enough act that Sandi did not object to at the time, though he wouldn't have done it himself. Still, it was an arrangement he would have been okay with her continuing. After Doreen had taken the wild dog into the house a couple weeks ago, the situation quickly became untenable. The dog had fully assimilated into the household and his wife had grown unnaturally attached to the beast. In his opinion, having it eat at the table with them and allowing it to sleep in their bed was just unacceptable. It had grown bold as a result, thus alienating Sandi. It apparently wasn't going anywhere, but neither was Sandi, who wasn't about to surrender his dominance or his home. It was him or the dog.

He knew he was getting close to his destination as he drove past the airport. The entrance to the trailer park was off one of the side roads. He was relying only on his limited knowledge of the area rather than GPS, avoiding use of all electronics to prevent cyber evidence that could later be traced to him. He didn't want to leave anything to chance in case things went sideways. He had played it safe the whole way. It was how he did everything. At that moment, no other soul even knew what he had planned; not even the third party he was going to contract to get rid of the animal.

As the neighborhood became seedier, he was glad he didn't take the Mercedes. The Volvo stuck out enough around this part of town. Fortunately, it was an overcast and moonless night and there was little in the way of street lighting. Even if someone identified the make and model, he had strategically secured a plastic bag around the rear license plate to conceal the tags. If the police pulled him over, it would appear that he had run over the bag, which had inadvertently wrapped itself around the plate.

The sign for Glad Tidings Estates was small and he almost missed it. He had used a computer at the library to find Brance's last known address. He pulled into the trailer park, surprised by how many residents were out and about. Sitting on porch chairs and benches, they looked up and stared as Sandi drove slowly through the park. A number of children were playing in the side yards near rusted heaps of old junk cars. He didn't like it, but he had to drive extra slowly to see the numbers on the homes. Some didn't have any at all. Then he saw it, a nondescript double wide with 99 affixed to the red vinyl siding near the front door, which was accessed by a set of simple wooden stairs. There was no attached porch like most of the other units. It looked fairly new, and in a lot better shape than the others in the park. It was adjacent to a neglected in-ground pool, half full of inky black water. The surrounding yard was overrun on all sides by tall weeds and enclosed by a sturdy chain link fence.

Sandi pulled his Volvo to a stop beside it and stepped out, pulling the tan briefcase out with him. As he approached the trailer, he was careful not to look around at anyone who might be watching him. He pressed the doorbell at the top of the stairs, listening to the muted chime inside. As he waited, he looked at the windows. The blinds were drawn, and he could not tell if any lights were on inside. He could feel his heart begin to race with nervous excitement. He was about the ring the bell again when the door parted slightly and a raspy voice from the darkness on the other side said, "Yeah."

"Are you Brance?" Sandi asked.

"What do you want?" the disembodied voice snapped back.

"I have a proposition for you."

After a lengthy pause, the door opened wider. "Come in. Close the door behind you."

Sandi entered without hesitation and was immediately struck by an offensive odor. It was the rank, ammonia-like smell of rotting fish, which he realized was coming from the two sets of muddy boots on the floor by the door and from the chest waders hanging from a coat rack on the near wall. The stench was so bad, Sandi reflexively coughed, nearly gagging.

"You get used to the smell," Brance said with a sense of satisfaction. He was tall, with distinctive Native American features; high cheekbones, almond-shaped eyes, and straight black hair that was beginning to thin and recede. Sandi recognized him immediately. “Have a seat,” the host told him.

There were a couple of ratty couches and a wooden chair arranged around a cheap, glass-topped cocktail table where a couple of scented candles burned. With no other source of illumination, the interior was shrouded in heavy shadow. Whatever the fragrance of the candle, it was overpowered by the fishy aroma. There was drug paraphernalia scattered across the tabletop, as well. A bald anemic-looking man with a neck tattoo sat like a statue on one of the sofas. He appeared to be sleeping, though he had a wide grin baked onto his face and a small glass pipe in one hand.

Sandi made his way across the roomy trailer, littered with snack food wrappers and empty whiskey bottles.

Brance dropped down onto the other sofa as Sandi sat in the chair opposite, placing the briefcase on the floor between them.

“Do I know you?” Brance inquired.

“We used to go to the school together,” Sandi said. “Olive Street Elementary.”

“Olive Street Elementary,” Brance repeated with a half-smile. “That was a long time ago.”

“I’m Sandi Diaz.”

Brance squinted back at him in silence.

"Sandoval. Sandoval Diaz."

Brance's eyes flashed with recognition. "Sandoval," he said, nodding. "I remember you. You were that smart kid who always sat in front. I think I remember hearing that you went on to some expensive boarding school for rich kids."

"Well, Creedmont is rather prestigious, I guess. But it's really diverse and inclusive. I'm Puerto Rican, right?"

"It's diverse around here, too." Brance said with a cackle. "I'm Native American. The only color that *really* matters, though, is green, ain't that right?"

"Yeah, I suppose so," Sandi concurred. He shot a brief glance over at the other man. "I was hoping we could talk alone."

"This is my associate, Declan. Whatever you have to say to me, you can say in front of him. Declan, say hello to Sandoval."

"Yo, Sandoval," Declan said, his voice slurred, his eyes half-lidded.

Sandi hesitated a moment. He did not make the other guy out as a cop, but he had to ask. If he *was* a cop, wearing such filthy clothes, stinking of brine, with dirt caked under his fingernails, same as Brance, he would have to be *deep* undercover. "Are you a cop?"

The two men looked at each other and started to laugh, then Declan relit the pipe. "What do you think, Sandoval?"

"Call me Sandi."

"Sandi, you kinda caught us at a bad time," Brance said. "We were about to get ready for work. So, tell me, and make it quick, what is it you came all the way out here from your ivory tower to ask me."

"I need you to do a job for me."

Brance gave a quick nod at the reeking gear by the door. "As you are quite aware, I already have a job."

"This is specialty job. Not much to it. The pay is good."

"What exactly are you looking for?"

"To be perfectly blunt, I want you to kill my dog."

The two men looked at each other and burst out laughing so hard this time that it produced a coughing fit in Declan that lasted for several moments before subsiding.

"You serious?" Brance asked. "You want to have your dog killed?"

"Yes," Sandi said soberly.

"Why can't you take care of it yourself? You could poison him, or something."

"Well, it's kind of a tricky situation," Sandi began. "To begin with, the dog doesn't like me. I won't be able to get that close. And I don't want my wife to think I had any involvement in it. I have to be well removed from this. It can't look suspicious."

"You want to make it look like an accident?" Declan asked and started coughing again.

"What makes you think I would even consider doing anything like that?" Brance asked.

"I heard that you, you know, did some stuff for the mob."

"You read about my arrest a few years ago, you mean. The charges all got thrown out of court for lack of evidence. Did you read that?"

"Yes, I know. Believe me, I know how crazy this sounds. I just need you to do this for me. It can't be traced back to you. Nobody even knows I'm here."

Sandi instantly regretted saying that. If this guy actually could take a life without remorse, here was an opportunity to kill someone and take what he surely knew by now was a briefcase full of money.

"How much you got in there?" Brance asked, acknowledging the case on the ground.

"Ten thousand in cash," Sandi told him. "That's just half of it."

"Twenty thousand to kill a dog. How'd you come to that price?"

"I did some research."

Declan chortled. "What did you do, *Google* how much a hired killer gets paid to kill a dog?"

"Of course not," Sandi said. He wasn't about to tell them that he had actually seen a rerun of a *Matlock* episode where a horse trainer paid someone $20,000 to kill his horse so he could collect the insurance money. Sandi hadn't pro-rated the money to today's dollars, but considering that this was only a dog instead of a horse, he thought the offer was more than fair. "But I can't go any higher with the money without raising some serious red flags," he added.

Brance hesitated. He looked at Declan, whose expression of silent approval was all too obvious. The two of them appeared to be in consensus, but what it was that they were agreeing to Sandi wasn't entirely sure at that moment.

"The other half will be waiting for you in the house when you go there to do the job," Sandi informed them. "I'll leave the money inside the visor of the knight by the staircase in the foyer. You can't miss it."

"I find this whole thing… what's the word I'm looking for?" Brance turned to Declan.

"Fucked up," Declan submitted.

"Presumptuous," Brance said. "See I know big words, too. Don't you think that's presumptuous of you, Sandi? Bringing money here, assuming that I would do something like that when you don't even know me. Some folks in my shoes might even take that as an insult."

"I don't mean to offend you," Sandi said evenly. "I only wanted to limit our interaction. As a lawyer, this would be safer for both of us. I didn't want to have to return with the money another time after coming to an agreement today. There's always more risk with increased contact. Who knows what might happen. I could return with the money and walk into a setup by local police or the FBI."

"So, not only do you assume I'm some kind of crazed killer for hire, but you think I'm a rat on top of it."

"I'm just trying to play it safe. That's all. Really."

Brance's watchful eyes studied him in silence. He seemed willing to listen, so Sandi continued.

"Tomorrow night my wife will be at her writing class downtown. She leaves the house around 5:30 and gets back around 8:30. That gives you a three-hour window. The money will be there. I can't leave the front door unlocked. That would be too much of a coincidence to explain away. But the ground floor windows are always open.

The kitchen, facing south, is your best bet. It's furthest away from the bedroom where the dog will be, and you'll be out of earshot. Do we have a deal?"

Brance took a long moment to consider the proposition, then extended his right leg and pulled the briefcase closer to him.

Chapter Two

She hadn't seen Susan in such a long time, and she didn't want the night to end before it started. However, she didn't know how much longer she could hide the pain she was feeling.

"I'm going to run to the ladies room before the food gets here," she announced and stood up.

"Again?" Susan asked, more concerned than surprised.

"I've been drinking a lot of water," Doreen told her. "I'll be right back."

She had been peeing a lot lately, but excessive intake of water wasn't the product of her discomfort. The water in the toilet was stained dark pink, which did not surprise Doreen after the bloody discharge earlier that morning.

When she was young, she could recall her mother complaining about bad periods, but Doreen never had any problems before, so she thought it was odd, and more than a bit worrisome to experience something like this now. She couldn't help wondering if something might be wrong. She didn't like thinking about it, but her mother died of ovarian cancer at about the age Doreen was herself right now.

She cringed as the constant throbbing in her lower abdomen intensified. Sitting helped with the back pain she had been experiencing, but she would have cried if someone had not entered the bathroom just then. However, instead of high-heeled footfalls, there was the distinctive clacking sound of thick nails on the floor, like the gait of a large four-legged animal.

That was impossible, Doreen told herself. What would an animal be doing wandering around a restaurant? Even if it was a service dog, there would be someone with it.

It's just your imagination, Doreen. You're stressing yourself out. Relax.

She closed her eyes and pursed her lips, breathing in and out slowly, hoping that would help her situation.

Whatever it was, it went into the stall right next to her. She didn't understand why anyone would do that when there were about ten other stalls, all of them empty. When you enter a public bathroom, you always look to see which stalls are occupied and leave at least a one-stall gap between you and anyone else. All you have to do is check for legs. Doreen had checked for legs. Why didn't this woman?

Doreen wiped, replaced her pad, and flushed. As she washed her face, she noticed how ashen her complexion appeared despite the makeup she was wearing.

Must be the lighting, she forced herself to believe.

Looking past her pallid reflection in the mirror, she saw the closed door of the stall next to the one that she had used. Under the stall door, instead of legs, there were animal paws, with dark black fur. The sound of a forceful spatter of liquid on the tile floor echoed around the bathroom as a large puddle of urine spread across the floor under several stalls.

Doreen blinked twice and then turned around to look at the stall head-on. Under the same stall now was a pair of nyloned feet wearing black sling back heels. She chuckled in relief, attributing that vision to the lighting, as well, and then returned to her table.

"Are your breasts tender?" Susan asked when Doreen sat down.

Doreen's eyes widened. "Excuse me?"

"Frequent urination is a sign of being pregnant. If your breasts are tender, you might want to think about stopping by the drugstore on your way home tonight to get a DIY test."

Doreen laughed uncomfortably. “I don’t think so.”

“You can tell me, Doreen. We’ve known each other since kindergarten.”

“There’s nothing to tell.”

“Last time we talked, you’d started taking Clomid.” She smiled cheerfully. “You remember Shanna Dolan? I still talk to her on occasion. She was taking Clomid and got pregnant with twins.”

Doreen broke eye contact. It was not out a sense of shame for not having conceived a child that she was unable to look at Susan. She knew that it did not make her less of a woman. Her desire to start a family was something she wanted to do for herself and for Sandi. Her inability to provide this to both of them made her sad, and she turned away because she did not want to cry in front of her friend.

“I didn’t have any luck with it,” she finally said. “I stopped taking it after a couple months.”

“Well, I wouldn’t give up. Lots of couples have trouble conceiving and there are other fertility drugs that might work for you.”

Doreen was slowly pulled under a wave of pain, which drowned out Susan’s voice. She knew her friend meant well, but she didn’t want to go deep into her personal life and admit that she and Sandi had given up trying to have children of their own. They were both getting too old, and now there were indications that she was heading hard and fast toward menopause. Adoption was something that had been talked about for all of five minutes. Sandi wanted to have *his* blood running through the veins of his children or he didn't want children at all. She hadn't even bothered bringing up the option of surrogacy to him.

Thankfully, the waiter appeared with their meals. He set a bowl of nutmeg broccoli soup down in front of Susan, followed by a roast beet root and pumpkin salad. For Doreen, he laid out two large plates, on one a stack of glazed short rips and on the second a grilled flank steak.

"That's a lot of meat," Susan commented when the waiter left. "Are you *sure* you're not pregnant?"

Doreen didn't know what had possessed her to order what she did, but she had absolutely no appetite now, and just looking at the food made her nauseous. She supposed that she hadn't been thinking clearly and wanted to bring home something for Sandi. Whatever her rationale, Susan realized that something was wrong with her friend. No longer able to keep her condition a secret, Doreen confessed to Susan that she was not feeling well, and she broke down crying in the process.

"You poor thing," Susan said. "You were feeling like this all night, and you didn't say anything?"

Doreen took a moment to dry her eyes and blow her nose. "I didn't want to postpone our night out," she said when she had herself composed. "We planned this months ago, and it's been forever since we've gotten together."

"We'll do something again soon," Susan promised, comforting her friend as they left the restaurant together, carrying the meals they didn't eat with them in doggie bags. The cars sent by the driver services they ordered were waiting for them out front by the curb.

As they were saying their final goodbyes, a scrawny dog came out of the alley behind the restaurant. It had matted gray fur and it's muzzle was crusted with a dark, greasy substance. The stray stopped momentarily, lifting its head and twitching its nose, as if picking up a scent. It fixed on Doreen and advanced toward her in a stealthy but determined manner. The animal, which normally avoided humans at all costs, moved intrepidly through a crowd of people with a singular focus. Just as the Doreen and Susan engaged in a parting embrace, the brazen dog approached Doreen from behind and raised its head, thrusting its snout forcefully up between her legs.

Feeling the urgency of the action, and the hot breath on her crotch, she let out a startled scream. The dog would not remove itself from her, even as she moved away. Everyone around turned and watched her distress with detached indifference. Finally, the restaurant valet intervened and tried to scare the dog away, but it remained firmly affixed to her. The back door of her car was open and when she made a sudden move to get inside, she managed to disconnect herself from the aroused canine. She quickly closed the door behind her before it could jump in with her.

"Let's go," she commanded.

The driver, an Asian-American man, looking at her with an amused grin on his face, nodded silently. As he pulled away from the curb, the dog pursued the electric vehicle as it eased into the slow-moving city traffic.

"Looks like your little friend is following you," the driver said. "Must be that meat of yours it wants."

"Excuse me," Doreen said, taking offense to the comment.

Her face flushed as she looked over at him. Then she realized she was carrying a greasy bag reeking of steak and ribs.

All of a sudden, a pack of dogs appeared and joined the gray cur. There were a half dozen of them at first, but before long there were ten, a dozen, and more, chasing after them and bounding up at the windows, barking. Their claws scraped the side of the car and their noses left wet smears on the glass.

"Hey, get down," the driver yelled at the dogs. "You're scratching the shit out of my car! Get down."

Doreen closed her eyes and held her hands over her ears. When she looked up, they were safely on the interstate and, to her relief, there was not a dog in sight. Feeling a dampness beneath her, she shifted in the seat and saw a spotting of blood on the beige vinyl. As surreptitiously as she could, she removed some tissue from her purse and wiped the blood from the seat, putting a thick wad beneath her and sitting on it until she was dropped off at home.

Chapter Three

The house was quiet. Sandi didn't expect Doreen to be back from dinner with her friend until sometime later that evening. He wanted to make sure he was alone when he secured the money for Brance inside the helmet of the medieval knight in the hallway.

The space in the helmet was smaller than he thought and he had trouble closing the visor around all the money stuffed inside. He was rearranging the bills so they would all fit when he heard the clacking of thick nails on the hardwood floor around the corner from the kitchen. Four heavy sets. Sandi thought the dog had been locked in the master bedroom down the hall, which was what Doreen normally did when she was out. But the sound grew louder, accompanied by the dog's ragged breathing.

Sandi remained perfectly still, and for a moment he couldn't move. Suddenly, he forced the visor down and then he removed the detachable broadsword from the knight's hand. He slowly walked backwards toward the stairs, holding the weapon out in front of him.

It had been dusk when he arrived, and he hadn't put on any lights, so it was dark in the house now, especially on this end, where all the windows faced east. As he ascended the stairs, he saw a dark shadow appear near the knight, where he had been standing a moment before. The canine's back came to about the height of the knight's tassets. A low growl started Sandi's heart racing in his chest. The curved staircase at his back gave him little advantage, and when the dog reached the landing and stopped, so did Sandi. Its large body was darker than the background. Only its eyes were visible. Even in the absence of light, they glowed red, as they would have in a photograph.

The growl grew louder and more intense.

"Delta." Sandi repeated the dog's name, using the gentlest tone possible. Speaking to a savage dog this way was supposed to calm the animal. However, it only seemed to further antagonize this one, making it snarl and bare its teeth. It was as if the dog didn't recognize him, despite its acute sense of smell.

"Easy, Delta. It's me."

He knew that the animal didn't like him, but it had never threatened him like this before. Suddenly realizing that he had never been alone in the house with the dog,

Sandi's concern turned to terror. Maybe it was somehow aware what he had planned for it, Sandi thought, and with Doreen out of the house, it was seeking to assert dominance. One thing was certain, Delta was strong enough to tear him apart.

In fear for his life, Sandi prepared to defend himself, pushing the pointed edge of the sword at the animal. "Stay back," he warned. "Back!"

Delta started to snap. The violent clacking of its teeth echoed around the foyer.

Suddenly a noise from the garage diverted the dog's attention. All of the canine's aggressive behavior stopped as it looked around toward the other end of the house. Its narrow, pointed ears perked up. A moment later the garage door in the kitchen slowly creaked open.

Oh, no!

Sandi wondered if Brance had gotten the day wrong.

Delta gave two sharp barks that were not threatening in the least and then excitedly headed toward the kitchen.

"I'm happy to see you, too, Delta."

It was Doreen. Every muscle in Sandi's body, on high alert from the adrenaline rush, sagged with relief at once. No longer able to support the weight of the five-pound sword, a blunt edge of the double blade weapon struck the riser near his feet. The lights snapped on and his wife appeared at the end of hallway. She started when she saw him, clutching a hand to her chest.

"Sandi?" she gasped. "You scared me half to death. Why are you sneaking around like that?"

"I wasn't expecting you to be home, either. Not this early. What happened?"

"Oh, well, Susan started to get one of her migraines while we were eating so we left early, and she went home to rest." Her eyes narrowed as she noticed the sword in his hand. "What are you doing with that?"

Sandi looked down at Delta, sitting innocently at Doreen's side. "That godforsaken animal of yours that you brought up from the depths of hell," he shouted, pointing with his other hand at the dog. "He tried to kill me."

"What? Delta?"

"Yes. That wild beast at your heels now. You should have left him outside, where all beasts belong."

"Who's calling who a beast?" Doreen asked, rubbing Delta behind the ears. "Look at the way you're acting, Sandi. Raising your voice and brandishing that sword like you're Charles the Great. What did you expect? He didn't know who you were or what you were doing. He was just defending his house." She stroked his muzzle. "Yes. Who's my good boy? You are." She bent down and let the dog lick her face.

"You're only further encouraging that kind of behavior, Doreen. And let me make it clear, this is not his house. It's mine. He's a guest here. And a temporary one at that, I might add."

"That's just what I mean, Sandi. You haven't made even the slightest attempt to be his friend. Ever since he's been here, you've treated him like an outsider. He knows that. And that makes him feel bad. He's a very sensitive, loving dog. You haven't given him a chance."

Sandi realized that what he was saying was only working against him. The last thing he wanted to do was fall under suspicion after the dog went missing. He had been working hard to contain his strong adverse feelings about cohabitating with the animal. He didn't want to blow it now, especially with what had been arranged to happen the following night. Doreen would be at the community college taking her creative writing class, and he would be working late when Brance and Declan showed up to ransack the house during an apparent robbery. The dog would disappear in the process and Sandi would be in the clear.

"I'm sorry, honey," Sandi began. As he made his way down the stairs, the dog didn't take his eyes off him. "You're absolutely right. I don't know what came over me. I'll try harder to be more welcoming." He made only the slightest motion to reach down to pet the top of Delta's head, but a menacing growl deep inside the dog's throat halted the attempt instantly.

"He needs to warm up to you, too," Doreen said. "It takes time. You never had any pets growing up. He probably senses that. You just have to show him that you care."

"Yeah, that's all it is."

"Now come on eat," Doreen said. "Susan and I went to Cadena's for dinner. I brought you home some ribs and some steak. Your favorites."

"Yum. That sounds good." He took his wife by the hand and gave her a kiss on the side of her lips. "Thank you."

She looked at him with an appreciative smile. "Thank you for trying so hard. I know this is not easy for you."

Feeling guilty about the deceit, Sandi wanted to dismiss the praise that he did not deserve. "Oh, come on now."

"No, seriously." She grasped the side of his head, behind his ears, and held him there as he tried to turn away. "Thank you." She pressed her full lips to his.

The dog's low growl persisted for the duration of the kiss, stopping when she released him.

"I think he's jealous," she said. "That's so cute. I'll give you kisses too." She bent over and let the dog lick her face.

Sandi turned away, placing the sword back in place in the knight's hand before following Doreen down the hallway toward the kitchen.

"See what you did to him," she said looking back at Delta, who remained where he was, sitting and looking up at the knight.

Sandi stopped and turned around.

That son of a bitch knows. What is it with this fuckin' animal?

"You got him spooked with that sword," Doreen said. "Come on boy, I'll feed you, too."

And with that, the dog jumped up on all fours and bounded into the kitchen with Doreen.

As usual, around Doreen, Delta's demeanor was good-natured. It was as if the dog was putting on some sort of deception for her benefit.

In much the same way he was deceiving her, Sandi thought.

The dog's tail was even wagging as it devoured the food in its bowl and then watched as Sandi ate his meal. He still felt uncomfortable as the dog stared at him. To Doreen, Delta's focus was the food, but Sandi wasn't buying that. The dog was looking directly at him with those evil eyes. Its irises were stippled light blue and pink, with dark pink pupils that made them appear red. They were unnerving and mesmerizing at the same time. The message that they conveyed to him was apparently very different than what they were communicating to Doreen. She saw a dog that was happy to be in the house, but to Sandi, Delta wanted something more; and not just to kill him, but replace him.

It was bizarre enough having those thoughts, but what made it even more unusual was the feeling Sandi had that the dog was well aware of everything that he was thinking. They were both doing their best to maintain a poker face, a game that continued when they turned in for the night. While the dog had previously been content to sleep on a roll of old blankets and a comforter on the floor beside the bed, the last few nights Doreen had allowed Delta to sleep with them. Sandi had objected each time, but he didn't say anything tonight. The Texas king mattress was plenty big enough for all three of them to fit comfortably. There was room to spare with the dog curled up at Doreen's feet.

They watched TV for a while, speaking very little. Doreen didn't mention the difficult time she was having with her period, and Sandi didn't divulge to her the extreme depths of fear and resentment he had for Delta. When Susan texted her to find out how she was feeling, and asked if she wanted to talk, Doreen texted back: *Feeling much better. Thanks. Call you in the morning.*

She wasn't lying to her friend. Her belly pain had subsided. Not only that, but she was feeling a bit playful, sexually. An increased libido was not something that had been a part of her menstrual cycle since she was very young. She thought she could easily dismiss the sexual prompts, but she found that she could not. She was swept away by them, and when she suddenly rolled to her side and kissed Sandi deeply and sensually, she was just as surprised as her husband.

This alerted Delta, who raised his head and began to growl deep in his throat.

Doreen initiated sexual congress, reaching into her husband's pajama bottoms and stimulating him with her hand. He became hard quickly.

"Doreen," he moaned softly.

Delta rose to his feet, still growling.

"Delta," Doreen admonished the dog as she continued.

"Yes, Doreen! Just like that."

Delta's growling grew louder.

"DEL-TA!"

"Don't stop," Sandi pleaded as her hand slowed.

"I'm sorry." Doreen pulled her hand out of Sandi's pajamas. "I can't do this with the dog here. Watching."

Delta stopped growling and slowly laid back down at the foot of the bed.

Before rolling back over to go to sleep, she kissed Sandi on the side of his face. "Goodnight."

She closed her eyes and soon drifted off to sleep. He watched TV for a little while longer before turning it off and closing his own eyes, though slumber did not come to him so easily. Thinking about what was going to happen the following night, he lay wide awake. He didn't think he would be able to sleep again until it was all over. To make matters worse, he was beginning to have serious doubts that he was handling it the right way. He realized he was putting his wife at considerable risk.

What if her class was cancelled and she was home when they showed up? What would they do to her?

He didn't know Brance or Declan. And he certainly couldn't trust them. He just wanted his peaceful home life back, but he may have only made things worse by initiating contact with the likes of Brance and his partner. He didn't like the way they looked or the way they smelled. There was something diabolical about them. He had a bad feeling about this, and he knew he had made a big mistake.

How dumb could I be?

He wondered if it was too late to call it off. He could go to them tomorrow and tell them to forget the whole thing, let them keep the ten grand for their trouble. It wouldn't resolve the domestic issue with Delta, but at least Doreen would be safe. It would be worth the financial loss.

What if they came to the house for the rest of the money anyway, he thought with dread.

And why wouldn't they? They were criminals, murderers, and God knows what else. The possible outcomes were too chilling to contemplate, but they still swirled around in his head. The mistake he made going down such a perilous path weighed heavy on him, and the burden became physical. He felt a strain in his chest, a tightness that constricted his breathing.

He groaned in distress, and when he opened his eyes he found himself staring directly into a pair of malevolent eyes glowing a fiery red in the darkness.

Delta was sitting on top of him. The dog's muzzle was inches from his face. Sandi froze. He tried not to move, but he began shaking with fear, and the harder he tried to remain still the more he shook.

The dog's nose wrinkled, exposing its upper teeth as a low growl escaped from the back of its throat. The animal's front claws began to slowly extend, the pointed tips digging into the sides of his neck, breaking the skin. A trail of blood dripped on the bedsheets. The force that Delta exerted on him felt like the weight of a two-hundred-pound man on his chest. Sandi was completely helpless.

As he peered into the dog's eyes, at length he felt a calmness wash over him and he stopped shaking.

Suddenly the dog pushed itself up, raking its claws down his chest in the process before slowly backing away, still growling.

Sandi seized the opportunity to peel the covers back and get out of bed. He found himself walking out of the bedroom, almost against his will. Delta, fully alert, watched him from the foot of the bed, its glowing eyes seeming to direct him away. When he was in the hallway, he wondered if it was a dream. Then Delta hopped off the bed and laid down across the threshold of the bedroom, and Sandi knew it was all too real.

Chapter Four

They had been at it for almost two hours. When Declan spotted the syphons of a geoduck clam peeking out of the mud, he would drop a small plastic disc over it, marking it for Brance, who would dig the alien-looking mollusk out the ground and leave it for Declan to collect. Brance was a machine when it came to harvesting these monster shellfish. The freakish geoduck was the largest burrowing clam in the world, existing three feet beneath the ocean floor, and it took some work to extract them. When he was high, as he was now, Brance could pull a half dozen of them out of the muck in an hour. He used an old garbage can with the bottom cut out to corral the underground delicacy, driving the galvanized steel cylinder down around the clam by laying a chunk of two-by-four over the top and stomping on it. His hands did the rest, pulling the sediment out of the tube one scoop at a time to free the sand-burrowing bivalve from its permanent residence.

Because of its giant neck, which was too big to fit inside its shell and extended out as much as three feet to feed on nutrients on the sea floor above, the geoduck was universally scoffed at for it phallic appearance. It was often referred to by such names as the dick clam, mud cock, or sea penis, among others. But this creature was a highly sought-after trade commodity, especially to eastern nations. A single puddle pecker of sufficient size might fetch up to three hundred dollars. It was like pulling money out of the ground.

The black market demand for geoduck was so great that it drew the interest of the local crime syndicate, who employed Brance to harvest the clams illegally, removing them from protected areas in numbers that far exceeded the limits set by state and federal agencies.

As the two men were finishing up their night's raid, the tide was on its way back in and the mudflat was filling with salt water. They had done well for themselves. Declan had filled the four large buckets with the colossal clams.

"Yo, dude," Declan called out. "We got our fill." He had to tell Brance when they were done, or he would keep on digging until he was underwater. "If you're done pulling pud, we should get the hell out of here."

"Relax," Brance said, smiling as he surveyed their present haul. "There's nothing to worry about."

But Declan was worried. The cartel they worked for was not to be trifled with. These were violent and dangerous men who were deadly serious about maintaining the lucrative revenue stream that geoducks generated for them in the world marketplace. The cartel paid a lot of money to officials with the Fish & Wildlife Service, the US Department of Agriculture, the EPA, and the Coast Guard to look the other way so that harvesters like them could illegally remove the clams that would then be smuggled overseas for a huge return on investment.

"Let's see what we got." Brance sloshed through the rising tide to inspect some of the specimens in the bucket. He laughed giddily as he handled some of the bigger ones. "This one's got to be five pounds." He giggled when it started to squirt water, and he turned the clam toward Declan, dousing him. "Clam cum," he laughed.

Declan was also uncomfortable with how much their little embezzling scheme had grown in recent weeks. It was one thing to make a few extra bucks on the side and do it safely so as not to get caught. But Brance had gotten greedy, skimming more and more of their take to sell at a steep discount to connections he had made. It was extremely dangerous. If the cartel got wind of what they were doing, they would both be killed and buried in the mud alongside the geoducks. They had come across several decomposed bodies that the cartel disposed of, and it was more unsettling for Declan each time they came across human remains. It was meant as a message to guys like them not to fuck with the cartel, and it was a message that Declan got loud and clear. He thought Brance was getting sloppy as well as greedy, and it troubled Declan enough that he felt he had to say something.

"Brance, man," Declan began. "I think we oughta cool it with the clams."

"What the fuck are you talking about?"

"Don't you think we made enough?" Declan inquired. "I mean, we don't need to be out here. We met our quota with the cartel. If they catch us out here, they'll wonder what we're doing. And that won't be good."

"You worry too much," Brance said dismissively. "They'll never find out."

"Yeah, well, we've come across other motherfuckers who thought the same thing, and now they're getting reamed by these mud-crawlin' dick clams."

"Don't give me that," Brance scolded Declan. "I don't remember you complaining about the extra 2K these things put in your pocket last week alone."

Brance was right about that. The money sure came in handy. Declan was able to afford some much-needed repairs to his motorcycle, and the high-quality heroin was really worth the additional outlay.

"It's just that we got more than enough already," Declan said. "We can't even get rid of what we have. They don't keep very long out of the ocean."

"I got a guy lined up who wants to buy whatever we have. We don't have inspectors on our payroll, so we have to be more cautious, and that takes a little more time. He should be here in a couple days with the money. The clams should keep until then. We'll get them packed for shipping the same day." He draped a wet, muddy arm around Declan's shoulders. "The only thing you should be thinking about is what you're going to spend your share of the take on after we get paid. Now, come one. Let's head back and do some celebrating."

Brance secured the handle of a bucket in each hand, and Declan grabbed the other two. They waded through shin-deep water as they headed back to dry land and their waiting van. The tide was coming in fast.

Declan could actually see it moving swiftly and rising. His anxiety rose along with it. Looking down, his imagination got the better of him and he thought he saw the outlines of rotting bodies beneath the surface. He needed a fix bad. He tried to keep his thoughts from wandering to the darker places where they often roamed, but he was helpless to redirect them. He envisioned himself lying in the mudflat, the water rising over his body, unable to move, the syphons of the geoduck clams opening all around him. His pulse quickened and his breath grew ragged as his nerves frayed, and he did what he normally did when he was nervous; he talked. Anything to distract him from the images that were flashing through his mind.

"Ya think that guy is for real, or what?" he asked Brance.

"What guy?"

"Your buddy from school. The one who wants you to kill his dog. Can you believe that motherfucker?"

"Oh, him. Yeah, he's always been a spoiled prick. But the money sure is real. And there's more waiting for us. A lot more."

They reached the edge of the beach where their van was parked. Declan looked over his shoulders to see if anyone was around, watching them. Someone from the cartel could be anywhere in the darkness, observing everything they were doing. He hurried to the van and placed the buckets he was carrying in the back. Brance followed with his.

"What did you mean, 'there's a lot more waiting for us?'" Declan asked from the passenger seat as Brance settled in behind the wheel. "The dude said there would be ten grand in the knight's helmet in the hallway."

"If he's willing to pay that much to kill his dog, how much do you think he'll pay us *not* to kill his wife," Brance asked. "People are always willing to pay a lot more for *not* killing than they are for killing. They'll give you everything they got to keep themselves or their family alive. It might be a jackpot. Who knows what we can pull out of there."

Declan hesitated. "If you extort more money from him, you'd have to be willing to kill him."

"Naturally," Brance said. "I never liked him anyway."

Declan turned away and rolled down his window to circulate the air and release some of the funk from inside.

"Do you have a problem with it?" Brance asked him.

"No, no, I just figured with all the money we'll be getting for the clams, we don't need to get involved any more deeply with a guy like that. I'm mean, the guy's crazy, right?"

"He's crazy rich, and he won't be expecting us tonight." Brance stared at Declan to gauge his reaction. "Be sure to bring that sick knife you just bought. You're going to get a chance to use it."

Declan was able to maintain a cold, unaffected countenance, though it wasn't from indifference. He was starting to crash, and he felt completely exhausted. "I need a little pick-me-up before I do anything," he admitted.

"Oh, I'm with you there," Brance said as he turned the ignition, firing up the battered cargo van. "We'll put these things away and then light a nice big bowl."

That prospect made Declan smile for the first time all night.

Chapter Five

The two men parked their car off the main road a half mile away and walked through the rear of the trailer park unseen and unheard; no small feat considering their formidable frames. One was bigger in size and in the scale of ferocity than the other, although a person who was being hunted by either of them would be found just as dead. Hector Manuel Castillo Chavez was built like a fire plug. Over the years, he helped the drug cartel dispose of hundreds of victims by dissolving them in acid. Alberto Jesus Mijares Hernandez was more like a fire truck. He was taller and meaner, performing his contract kills like they were personal. He had committed over eight hundred murders, sometimes beheading and dismembering the victims.

They worked their way over to Brance's trailer, removing the Five-SeveN pistols they had been concealing. This Belgium-made semi-automatic was the weapon of choice for many cartel members. The 5-7 was known as a "cop killer" as its bullets could easily tear through a protective vest. Because the ammunition is light, it exits the barrel at a very high velocity. The projectile tumbles when it hits a target, ripping a large hole in the victim, similar to the M-16 rifle. It holds a twenty-round magazine, plus an additional round in the chamber; in the hands of these extremely dangerous men, this meant that there was no possibility of escape.

Hector walked around to the front door while Alberto found a rear entrance. At almost the same instant, they leveled their broad shoulders and impacted the respective doors. The locks were no match for their bulk. The strike plates exploded out of the door jambs, the frames shattering. Dressed entirely in black, they entered the trailer like shadows. They paused inside and listened carefully, but there was no sound. If someone had been home, there would have been frantic movement, accompanied by terrified voices or heavy breathing, but it remained quiet and still. They did a quick search of the residence and determined what they already knew. The men they were looking for were not there, but the killers did not relax. They still had a job to do. It just involved more work, looking for clues and locating the subjects as quickly as possible, then murdering them.

They met in the living room, where Alberto flipped on a floor lamp. The remains of a partially eaten geoduck, still in its shell, was stretched across most of the living room table, accounting for the terrible smell.

Hector looked over at Alberto and grimaced with disgust that the two men had been eating the thing raw. Alberto reached down and touched the glass pipe resting on the table. The bowl was still a bit warm. He nodded to Hector, who lifted the pipe and held it to his nose. His sniffed deeply several times and then dabbed a finger into the gooey white substance in the bowl. Bringing it to the tip of his tongue, he tasted it. The vinegary smell and pungent bitter taste were unmistakable, and along with the color, Hector easily identified it as high-grade heroin.

"It's not cut as much as that shit they usually get," Hector said. "They ain't buying this on what they're getting paid. Not living here and riding those tricked out bikes."

The cartel suspected that Brance and Declan were doing some side dealing, harvesting geoduck and selling some for their own personal profit, which was a big no-no. It was more than just a murderable offense. Under these circumstances, the killing had to be carried out as violently and with as much pain as possible. The bodies would then be displayed, left out in the open to be seen by the public as a way to deter other employees from engaging in this kind of profiteering at the expense of the cartel.

The two clammers had first fallen under suspicion when Declan began buying high end heroin from the same cartel dealers that they had been buying their regular heroin from. The sudden taste for the high-quality dope meant they had some extra money to spend. That's all it took to put them on the cartel's hit list. Even if the accusation turned out to be false, and clam diggers weren't selling product behind the cartel's back, it didn't matter. Their lives were expendable, and they could easily be replaced. The work they did would be done by someone else. Besides, Hector and Alberto needed to work, too. And they enjoyed killing folks. There didn't have to be a reason.

They began to search the trailer methodically, one room at a time, looking for anything that would help them locate the men. The place was such a mess to begin with, it looked like someone had already gone through it. Alberto wondered if the two men had gotten wind that the cartel was on to them. Perhaps they had worked themselves into such a state of paranoia and fear over their smuggling activities and drug use that they blew town with their lives and whatever money they made on their little enterprise. It was a possibility that had to be considered.

There were two sides to every deal, and finding evidence of that relationship was just as important. Getting the name of the buyer, whoever Brance and Declan were selling the clams to, and then tracking that person down to assassinate, as well, would be a bonus. A gruesome crime scene displaying this body would go a long way to instill terror and prevent others who might thinking of working side deals with cartel employees. It was all about messaging, yet as far as Alberto could tell, no matter how harsh the torture or how brutal the death, it never seemed to be clear enough. Even after all the people he alone had killed at the behest of the cartel, there was never a shortage of contract killing assignments. In fact, he was only getting busier. And he was just one enforcer. You would have thought by now, with the ability to instantly access information and view endless news loops and images of cartel violence, there would be nobody stupid enough to fuck with such a vast and ruthless criminal organization. But there was always someone whose greed and stupidity superseded logic and reason, numb nuts who put their very lives at risk for a little bit of money. In this case, there were at least two drugged-out ignoramuses trying to get away with something. Tomorrow there was sure to be two more, and every day, all month, year after year, into eternity. And that was all right with Alberto.

After they had combed over the whole house and turned up nothing but drug residue, empty whiskey bottles, and assorted trash, the two hit men looked at one another, perplexed. As Alberto paced across the living room floor, his leather cowboy boots clacked on the faux wood under his heels. Suddenly, his footfalls become muffled as he stepped on a section of flooring that was a slightly lighter shade than the rest. He stopped and looked down, tapping his right foot on the floor. It made a dull, hallow sound. Bending at the waist, he felt along the ground for a hidden seam. His fingernails caught on a narrow gap, and he pulled gently upward. A wedge of the floor swung open on a hinge revealing a secret cubbyhole.

"Jackpot," Alberto said.

A tan briefcase was laying atop a stash of white plastic trash bags. Alberto removed the briefcase while Hector fished out the garbage bags and emptied their contents of loose bills onto the floor. They were in small denominations, mostly $10s and $20s but some $5s and even $1s. Many of the notes were crumpled and dirty, not bound in any way, but haphazardly collected and tossed in the bags. It was difficult to estimate just how much was there, but it wasn't enough to die over. Certainly not enough to die over.

"What are they doing, selling these things wholesale at the farmers' markets?" Hector said with a little laugh. "These are all small-time buyers."

Alberto popped open the briefcase, which contained ten neatly banded $1,000 stacks, all in $100 bills. "Not this guy," he said. "Ten grand here, maybe another five there on floor." He dropped the open briefcase onto the dingy couch and started to go through the inner pockets, not expecting to find anything, but then his fingers touched something, which he promptly removed. It was a business card.

"Sandoval Diaz, esquire," Alberto read out loud.

Hector smiled. "We got our guy."

"He lives in Denny-Blaine," Alberto said. "66 Prospect Street."

Denny-Blaine, a residential neighborhood in one of the most affluent and exclusive regions in Seattle, was dominated by mansions of varying architectural styles built in the early 20th century, many of which are situated on extremely large urban lots.

"We don't know what we're going to run into there," Hector began. "Or what he has for security. It could be a big job. If we're going to go at these people hard, make an example of them, we could use some extra hands."

"You're right," Alberto agreed. "We'll make a few calls and head over there tonight to take care of all of them."

"Yeah, we'll show 'em they fucked with the wrong people."

"Let's grab this money and make some calls from the car," Alberto said. "We'll try El Lagarto first. Maybe Almeja."

"Don't forget El Ratone," Hector said. "I've worked with him in the past. He has a decapitation crew and a van to transport the remains to any drop off location."

"Right," Alberto agreed as he snapped the briefcase shut. "We'll use him. You have his phone number."

Hector crammed all the cash into one trash bag and slung it over his back like some gangster Santa Claus.

"Take those empty garbage bags," Alberto instructed him. "We can use those to put their hands and heads inside and leave behind for the police to find."

They left through the backdoor with the cash.

On their way back to the road, Alberto suddenly halted as his nose wrinkled in response to a familiar smell that had an extra funk to it. "Wait a minute," he said.

Hector stopped beside him and got a whiff himself. "What the fuck!"

Alberto nodded toward the abandoned swimming pool. "What wrong with this picture?" He was indicating the optics of a brand new enclosure around a pool that did not look like it had been in use for a very long time.

They moved to take a closer look at it. Alberto handed the briefcase to Hector and climbed over the fence with ease. Peering directly down into the pool, he could tell that it contained more than just standing water, but a dark, mud-like sediment. On the ground beside him was a heavy-duty steel pole with a deep net bag. He picked it up and stuck it into the muck, forcing it below the surface. He didn't have to go down very deep before he came into contact with something. He struggled to move the object, but he kept working until he freed it up enough to secure it in the net and pull it to the surface. Raising it up out of the pool, he dropped it to the ground by his side. Caked in mud was a small geoduck. It did not look well, and it smelled worse. If it wasn't dead already, it was dying. The mollusk embezzlers had made a makeshift holding tank for the clams.

They didn't need any more proof to know what Brance and Declan were up to, and it was all the justification they needed to kill both of them and anyone they were working with.

"A lot of heads and hands can fit in that pool with those clams," Hector said from the other side of the fence.

When Alberto nodded, it was as good as done.

Chapter Six

Delta was what he was being called now, but he had no name. He was unnamable. Most often he was referred to as Dog Man. Some would say he and others like him were an abomination. And maybe that was true, but it didn't matter. His only desire was to survive. There was nothing else. There was only this moment, and to continue to the next one required guile, intelligence, adaptation, fortitude, and brutality. In that regard, he was no different than any other living creature, doing whatever it takes to get to the next moment.

Although he was genetically half man, the humans he came in contact with either despised him or were horrified by his very existence. And all of them turned a cold shoulder on him, dismissing him as unworthy of kindness or affection. The woman they found was different, however. She was more than special. She was essential. Even if her compassion was rooted in something she did not understand, the gesture she made by providing food and shelter to him made their union all the more inevitable, and fateful. She truly did not know how special she was, though she would very shortly. He would have tried to explain it to her if he could, using her language. However, although he had the ability to change shape temporarily, into a more human form, his kind had lost the ability to speak long ago.

While Dog Man did not know the exact origins of his race, it was not something he ever thought about. He only knew that the numbers of his kind had been declining steadily for a long time. Indeed, with no other females left to mate with, this species of half human-half dog was on the verge of extinction, and it would only survive if he could mate with a descendant from the original bloodline that begot this race of chimeras. He had been wandering the lands for what seemed like an eternity in search of such a woman, and finally he found one. He had picked up on her scent, in part due to luck, but his persistence brought him within range of the pheromones she excreted. They were strong many miles away. He had followed the chemical trail to her home, now he was in her bed and she was in estrus. He knew what needed to be done.

It was time, Dog Man thought. The fishy smell was strong, much too intoxicating to resist any longer. Suddenly rising from the bed, he jumped down onto the floor. He slunk over to the bedroom door and stopped. Sticking his nose into the hallway, he sniffed deeply. He wanted to be sure that the human man was not around.

Earlier, using an ability he had with his eyes, a form of mesmerism, Dog Man had suggested that the man leave the room. Although he had, there was no way of knowing how long it would last. If the man was willful enough, and wanted very strongly to do something to interfere, he could break the trance. It was time to act.

Dog Man did not get a trace of the man, or anything else for that matter, being as close as he was to the woman's overpowering scent. Although Dog Man's senses told him that the man did not want him in the house, he did not fear for his life. He also intuited that the man was not inherently vicious or violent, like some humans, but he did detect that the man was up to something. Dog Man did not expect the man to simply abandon the woman without a fight, but at least he was not in the room now, and that alone made this moment all the more perfect for Dog Man to mate with the woman. They needed to breed in order to sustain a dying race.

Dog Man paced around the room, stopping to spray drops of urine in numerous locations, marking his territory to let the others know who was in charge. He would call the rest of the pack to join him in the mating. It would be after he mated with her first, of course.

Dog Man jumped back up onto the mattress and slowly worked his way up from the foot of the bed to where Doreen lay sleeping. Dog Man stopped and stared at her, breathing in her scent. Combined with the smell of the urine that filled the room, he became fully aroused. Slowly she opened her eyes and looked back at him, startled at first, but a moment after her eyes locked on his, he knew he had the woman.

***

Outside, in the section of woods behind the Denny-Blaine estate, the other dog men waited, tired, hungry, and horny as hell. There were only four of them, a pack with no females, and they knew of no others of their kind existing anywhere in the world. They were it. That's why what was taking place inside the big house was so important. Once the pack's alpha began mating with the woman, they would be signaled by their leader to join him in a last-ditch effort to repopulate their race.

They bided their time hunting for small game, a little playful wrestling, and sleeping. But mostly sleeping. It used up too much energy to hunt and play, energy they did not have, and wanted to save for mating.

They were dirty, they smelled bad, and they were scrawny compared to Delta, the alpha in the group, who always ate first and as much as he wanted until he was sated. He may as well have been king, there were no others who could even challenge him for that position. However, not all of the remaining dog men were happy to wait.

The pack had a natural hierarchy. Zoologists and other experts on animal behavior had come up with a ranking system to label each dog's social standing within their group, and it was more than accurate. This pack conformed precisely to this ruling system model. The second ranked dog in the pack, the alpha-beta, spent a majority of the time sitting alertly near the edge of woods, which the alpha had heavily marked with urine. The Number Two dog kept a constant watchful eye on the house, waiting for the signal. He didn't want to miss it. He knew his place, and he was comfortable enough in his role, but he wanted his share. He thought he deserved more than he was getting. He didn't like getting sloppy seconds during feeding or mating time. The alpha always got the best garbage from the trash, the choice meat and innards from a fresh kill or animal that was already dead, while the rest of them had to scavenge for leftovers, having to make do with decaying flesh or feces. While humans find such nourishment to be repulsive, excrement actually contains both the dead and living bodies of millions of bacteria, which made it a perfect source of protein, essential fatty acids, fat-soluble vitamins, minerals, antioxidants, enzymes, and fiber. The dog men didn't know any of that, of course, it just tasted really good. But even shit was in short supply for this hybrid breed of human and canine.

The woman used to come out and leave food. Although the alpha got most of it, there were always some crumbs left behind. But ever since their leader was allowed into the house, she stopped coming out with food. It had been many days since they had eaten anything at all besides a few stray beetles and caterpillars. They even resorted to chomping on some wild grass and herbs to sustain them while they awaited the call from their leader alerting them that the mating process had begun. The woman was already in heat, they could all smell it in the air. But the alpha hadn't begun mating with her yet, they could smell that too, and the alpha-beta dog was growing impatient. He was considering approaching the house and finding a way to get inside himself. He would not wait much longer.

The beta dog was the third in command. He was not necessarily a follower of the alpha, and he was apt to avoid confrontation and risk. He was the oldest in the clan, and for the most part kept to himself. By contrast, the beta-omega was the youngest and the most energetic, always going full throttle. He would chase his own tail for hours until he just conked out.

The omega, the lowest ranking dog in the pack, not surprisingly was the smallest and weakest among them. He was fearful and submissive. The only energy he showed was the nervous variety. Every time it would thunder during a rainstorm, he would shake uncontrollably.

The alpha-beta had the best sense of smell in the pack by far. He had the olfactory function of a bloodhound. Because this breed of dog had a smell range 1,000 times stronger than that of a human, it was referred to as 'a nose attached to a dog.' This heightened sensitivity was a skill that the Number Two dog used to his full advantage as the sentry in the pack.

As he sat watching the house, the scent of the woman grew stronger. Then suddenly he began to pick up on another scent. One that was unfamiliar, though not in the least unpleasant. It was a genuine fishy smell, like the kind he remembered from garbage bins in back alleys behind restaurants along the docks. It was still far away, but it was getting closer. The three dogs behind him were completely clueless about what was coming. One was fast asleep, one was shaking as gusty winds rattled the trees causing the limbs to creak, and one was licking his balls. The alpha-beta sat vigilantly at the edge of the woods, savoring the aromatic sex pheromones of the woman, ready to make his move.

Chapter Seven

When Doreen fell asleep, the sexually charged feelings that had suddenly awakened in her took wing. They carried her away to place where she felt no guilt or shame at all about not only her strong physical desires but also her menstrual cycle, both of which seemed to be intrinsically linked. Beyond the mess and the pain, her periods were often inconvenient and annoying, and they had always caused her some sense of embarrassment, even as an adult. When she was young, she never asked her mother any questions about what was happening to her body. Growing up in a house with strong religious convictions, it was not something that was talked about. After all, it had to do with sex, coming of age, the awakening of the woman inside her, of desire, the attraction of men and the dangers that it wrought – in particular, becoming pregnant. As a young woman, that might have been Doreen's biggest fear of all. She had been made to feel that getting pregnant was something that would have brought her great personal humiliation and dishonor to her family. Her grandmother told her it was a sin. Her mother's mother, a strict Catholic Italian woman, lived with them for a short time before she died. She would go to church virtually every morning, taking Doreen with her whenever possible, thinking it would keep her granddaughter pure.

In recent years, Doreen couldn't help wondering if the difficulty she had getting pregnant had to do with her upbringing and the deep Catholic guilt that had been instilled in her regarding ovulation, sex, and pregnancy.

She could vividly recall the trauma of her first period. She was only nine years old when she discovered blood on her underwear. She thought something was wrong and she ran crying to her mother, who took her straight to the drugstore to buy tampons. When they got home, her mother brought her into the bathroom. Without saying a word, her mother handed her the box and then walked out, leaving Doreen alone, as if expecting that her pre-teen daughter would know what to do with them by some innate feminine intuition. Every month after that her mother would just place the tampons in the bathroom closet. She even left them in the bag they came in from the store so that her father and brothers wouldn't have to see them.

Other people, especially men, acted differently if they knew she was on her period, so she tried to hide it. Most never knew, but sometimes some of them seemed to sense it. If she ever said anything out of character got angry or emotional and cried, they would accuse her of 'being on the rag,' and a lot of the time they were right. She would blush and turn away, feeling like she had done something wrong, imagining that they were laughing at her even if they were not.

In the midst of a dream now, she was alone in the woods. She didn't have any clothes on, and she was menstruating, but she felt no shame. It felt totally natural. As she walked, she left a trail of blood on the forest floor. Suddenly from behind came the sound of movement, something slinking through the underbrush, tracking her. She kept walking, and the sound got closer. She was not afraid, however. For the first time, she realized the power she held. As the one being chased, *she* was the one who was actually in control. When she was ready, she would stop and allow herself to be taken. It was liberating.

With a playful laugh, she started to walk faster, picking up her pace slowly until she was running, gamboling through the forest, zigzagging around trees and ducking under low hanging limbs. She reveled at hearing the heavy, frustrated breathing of her pursuer. If it wasn't so much fun, she might have felt sorry for what she was doing. It was rather pathetic for anyone to be so enslaved by a desire that it was literally leading you around by the nose, she thought as she giggled to herself.

When she had enough of the game, she slowed her pace before stopping altogether beside the trunk of a broad tree that had been sliced clean through, presenting itself like a wooden altar in the cathedral that was this sacred forest. Hearing the approach from behind, the ragged breathing, she draped her arms across the tree stump and bent over. She smiled and closed her eyes as a hirsute body pressed up against her hips and ass while two sinewy arms pushed her chest flat against the stump. She was unable to move as thick, blunt nails carved welts into the flesh of her back. The hot breath on her neck was pungent with anticipation. As Doreen was penetrated, she cried out, but with each thrust her cries diminished until she was moaning softly to the animal rhythm of the mating.

"It's a sin," a voice deep in the most primitive part of her brain whispered. When she heard it again, she looked up, realizing it was not coming from inside her head. It was her grandmother's voice. Then, from the woods to her right, her grandmother emerged. She was naked and the inside of her thighs were streaked with blood.

"Grandma!" Doreen yelped, deeply embarrassed for her grandmother. "What are you doing? Put some clothes on."

"It's a sin," the old woman repeated in broken English as she stopped and stared at her granddaughter, and the act she was engaged in.

Doreen's shame now reverted to herself, both familiar and profound. This traumatic emotion triggered a physical response, and she could no longer enjoy the sexual encounter she had been experiencing, even if it was only in a dream. However, the physical sensations felt real, so did the pain. It hurt more than any sexual encounter she ever had.

"Peccare contro Dio," her grandmother said, alternating her proclamation of sin in Italian as well as English.

Unable to move and stop what was happening, Doreen wanted to scream, but a bony hand covered with whisps of long, matted hair wrapped across her lips, sealing her mouth shut.

It was at this moment that Doreen realized she wasn't dreaming.

***

Sandi's eyes fluttered open as he awakened suddenly from an unusual state of unconscious that was somewhere between a dreamless sleep and a barbiturate-induced coma. Initially he had no mental recall, unaware of the time of day or where he was. He knew he was in bed and in an unfamiliar room that was exceedingly hot. The bedsheets shrouded around him were damp with perspiration. He struggled to untangle himself and then laid there a moment, allowing the air being circulated by the ceiling fan above to cool him down a little. Suddenly he realized that he was in one of the guest bedrooms upstairs. The air conditioning wasn't on, but he saw that the window was open, and humid summer air was streaming in through the screen.

He tried to push himself up into a sitting position, but his limbs were too weak. His entire body felt like it was slowly waking up, as if he had been under anesthesia.

Finally, he managed to sit up, which required much more effort than it should have. Reclining against the headboard, he wondered why he was there and what had happened. Then, outside in the distance, he heard a yodeling type howl, as if the animal was trying to communicate. After a few moments it stopped, and was answered by another dog, then another, and another, in unison, and all sounding like they were coming from the same area. Suddenly it occurred to Sandi what was responsible for all this, even if he didn't know the 'how' or the 'why.'

It was that dog.

His memory was foggy, but with each passing moment it became clearer. He had been with Doreen in their bedroom. They had been watching some television, clicking around the stations but couldn't find anything interesting, so they settled on the local news. Then Doreen initiated sex. Completely out of the blue, she started giving him a hand job, which surprised him more than anything. It was not something that had been on his mind, particularly with everything that he had set into motion regarding Delta. However, his wife's passion seemed extraordinarily intense, and it turned him on to see her in that state, the way she looked at him, the pattern of her breathing. He hadn't seen her that aroused since the time when they were trying to have a baby.

But before they could get very far, Delta interfered, and she just stopped. He had been cock-blocked by the damn dog!

That wasn't even the most troubling part, he realized. He ended up in the spare bedroom somehow. That part remained hazy. He closed his eyes and held the tips of his fingers against both sides of his temples like some kind of mentalist trying to attain a prophetic vision of the future, but nothing came to him. He could not remember a thing. He had closed his eyes and fallen asleep in his own bed and somehow woke up here. He tried to think his way through it, but it didn't make sense. He wouldn't have left his own bedroom and come up here voluntarily. So how else could he have gotten up here? The dog couldn't have dragged him upstairs by his collar with its teeth. And Doreen wasn't strong enough to carry him. But the question that bothered him the most about it was not the 'how,' but the 'why.'

What possible reason could there be for anyone to have done this to him?

He had a feeling the answer was right downstairs, although he was not quite strong enough to get out of the bed at that moment. Like his memory, his strength seemed to be returning slowly. Whatever had incapacitated him, it was wearing off.

Sandi's only comfort at that moment was knowing that by this time tomorrow, the dog problem at least would be resolved.

Just one more day, and it would be done.

Outside, the wild dogs began howling again, altogether, and with a different pitch, one that seemed to warn of impending danger.

Chapter Eight

There were security cameras mounted on the front gate, which Brance determined were dummies, but there was no sense taking any chances. He and Declan cased the property, which was bounded on three sides by a ten-foot stucco wall. The back yard was open, blending into what passed for the wilderness in Seattle; a small tract of trees. It wasn't worth walking all the way around so Brance and Declan found an access point along the south corner of the estate, where there were only two dark windows looking out at them. Beside that section of wall there was a narrow, branchless tree which the two of them were able to shimmy up with relative ease, before bounding atop and then over the wall. No sooner had their feet hit the ground when a high-pitched howling coming from multiple animals resonated through the otherwise peaceful night like a siren. Their vocalizations continued, going back and forth between them like a conversation.

Declan's eyes were as wide as saucers. "Yo, are those wolves?"

"Don't be stupid," Brance told him.

"It *sounds* like wolves."

"There aren't any wolves here. Not in Seattle. Probably just wild dogs."

"Are you sure?" Declan pulled his K-Bar from the scabbard tucked under the vest jacket he was wearing as he turned and peered into the woods at the far end of the property.

"Put that thing away," Brance told him. He grabbed Declan's jacket and held it open, trying to get his friend to sheath the 7-inch military combat knife. "Save it for what we have to do inside."

Declan finally did as Brance suggested, but only after the howling had ceased. "I hate wolves," he said.

"Dogs evolved from wolves," Brance informed him. "Dogs are basically domesticated wolves."

"What did you have to go and tell me that for?"

"Oh, just forget it."

"I can't *now*, yo" Declan whined. "I don't like this, man."

Brance didn't want to say anything, but suddenly he had a bad feeling about this scheme himself. He regretted getting involved, and he blamed Sandi for initiating the whole thing, projecting all his anger and fear onto the man who thought he could buy him for $20,000 in two installments. Getting back at Sandi was the only thing that compelled him to finish what he started. Well, that, and the other ten grand.

"Let's go," he said, and led the way toward the front of the luxury two-story brick home, where not a single light appeared to be on.

"Would you look at the size of this place, yo," Declan exclaimed. "When you said he had money, you weren't kidding. How much you think a spread like this goes for? A couple million?"

"A couple more than that," Brance replied.

"Damn! I wonder what it's like to be that rich."

"You'll never have to worry about it." Brance came to a sudden stop. "Quiet now," he whispered, then stepped cautiously into the mulch bed beside a dark window. "Get down." Declan ducked and moved over beside him. Taking a glance inside, Brance saw the outlines of a refrigerator, stovetop, and other kitchen appliances. He considered the possibility that no one was home, and that Sandi hadn't gotten around to putting the money in the knight. To his surprise, the thought came as a relief to him. It may have been the only way out of this now. He wasn't particularly looking forward to being involved in any real bloodshed. He was carrying his own Vietnam-era bowie knife, which had belonged to his father, but it was mostly for show. The weapon was one of the few possessions that he got from his dad, who had developed cancer and died ten years after returning home from the war. His father handled the toxic herbicide, Agent Orange, while serving in the Air Force. The blade was tarnished with age, but it was plenty sharp and lethal enough to slash a dog, a woman, and a doughy lawyer to death, but he didn't want to use it. That's why he made sure Declan was fully wired, having him smoke a full bowl on his own, while Brance only put the pipe to his lips, pretending to inhale. Whatever shit went down here tonight, Brance understood that it had to happen before the euphoric effects of the heroin started to fade and Declan became drowsy.

Brance tried the window and it was open, just as Sandi had promised it would be. They crawled inside one at a time, Declan behind Brance, who eased himself down from the countertop onto the floor. He held out an arm in front of Declan to ensure that he remained still and quiet while he listened for any sounds. There was only the soft hum of the refrigerator's electric motor. If not for the display lights on all the gadgets, it would have been as black as a tomb. As Brance stepped lightly across the tiles, the flare of a bright light suddenly illuminated the room. Brance froze in mid stride, expecting to confront one of the homeowners. But it wasn't Sandi or his wife entering the kitchen for a midnight snack, it was Declan.

"Shut that door," Brance quietly commanded when he turned and saw his partner's body stuffed halfway inside the fridge. "What are you doing?"

"I'm hungry, yo," Declan said as he turned around with chocolate on his face and a hunk of cake in his hand. "They got cake. You should see all the food they got in there. You want a beer?"

"No, I don't want a beer." Brance's voice rose in anger. "Are you trying to fuck this thing up? Close it, now."

"Okay, okay." Declan shut the door and the room returned to near total darkness.

"Let's focus on what we're doing here," was all he said, and then walked through the open doorway into a short hallway. Declan trailed behind him, cake crumbs dropping out of his mouth as he chewed.

When they reached the foyer, Brance spotted the knight in deep shadow by the staircase. For a split second, however, it didn't look like a statue to him. It had the appearance of some kind of beast, a creature that was part human and part something else. He approached it cautiously, pausing with his hand on the visor. Everything hinged on what was behind it. He lifted it slowly, and before it was all the way up, he knew they were in it for keeps when a couple hundred-dollar bills were dislodged and drifted to the floor.

Declan laughed. "Shit, yo. It's fuckin' all here. But we ain't got nothin' to put it in."

"All right, we'll grab a pillow from a bed and fill it," Brance said.

"Good idea." Declan eyed Brance gravely and started to reach under his vest. He paused, holding his hand there for a moment, waiting for approval. "Now?" he asked.

Brance nodded.

When Declan's hand came out of his coat, he was clutching the impressive tactical knife. It had a sinister black blade with a clip point and a partially serrated edge. Declan held it out in front of him, his other hand raised with the wrist turned inward, and his chin slightly tucked down like he was going into battle.

Brance gestured for him to start down the opposite hallway first. He kept his own knife safely tucked away. He didn't believe he would need it, not to defend himself against some rich guy's little mutt. Declan could take care of that. And Sandi didn't seem like the gun-for-protection kind of guy, so Brance didn't think he had to worry about getting shot in self-defense.

This hallway was longer, traversing a large wing of the house. There were multiple rooms on both sides. The doors stood open. They approached slowly and with great caution, pausing to sneak a look inside each room before moving on. They passed a study, a game room, an exercise room, and a home theater.

When Brance saw Declan's draw drop, he quickly put an index finger to his mouth and emphatically raised his eyebrows to keep Declan from voicing some expression of awe at the amenities enjoyed by Sandi and his family. Then he motioned Declan to continue forward. There was another room that was used for storage, containing boxes and various pieces of furniture. And then they came to the end of the hallway and a closed door. They stopped in front of it, and as they stood there in silence, they could hear a soft, rhythmic thumping sound coming from inside the room. They turned and looked at each other for a moment before Brance gave the go-ahead.

Declan raised the knife higher, holding it firmly, then took a deep breath and reached for the door handle. The door inched open slowly, revealing only darkness. The thumbing sound was louder now, and as their eyes adjusted to the dark, they were able to make out the outline of a large bed. On top, a shadowy form was thrusting repeatedly against the vague contours of what appeared to be a woman beneath it. Brance and Declan were behind the figure, whose back was to them and who was unaware of them standing in the doorway.

Declan grinned and held back a childish giggle. “They’re doing the devil’s dance, yo,” he said softly.

Suddenly, the figure on the bed whipped it’s head around at them. Though there was no light to create that red eye effect, they were shining with their own sanguine radiance. Declan had a better view than Brance, and what he saw did not jibe. He tried to connect the image of the man who had shown up at the trailer park with what he was seeing in front of him now. This man was taller, lean, but with dense muscle. He also appeared to be extremely hairy, though Declan couldn’t be sure that this wasn’t just some illusion of the shadows. All of a sudden, he got the distinct impression that what was looking back at him was not even human, and then it opened its mouth, exposing long canines and growling fiercely. Enough ambient light reflected a monstrous face. It had a wide, thick head and a wrinkled nose at the end of a short snout. Loose skin dangled from the side of its face, dripping thick, frothy saliva. The hair around its head was shorter and lighter in color than the hair on the rest of its body.

Declan immediately thought werewolf and screamed. When he did, the creature leaped off the bed and disappeared into dark shadow on the far side of the room, out of view. The woman on the bed didn't move.

"What the fuck!" Declan screeched. "Did you see that?"

"I don't know what I saw," Brance said.

"Where did it go?" Declan asked. "I don't see it." He squeezed the knife tighter, holding it out in front of him, too petrified to move. Brance stayed close beside him.

Suddenly, a shrill, urgent howl resounded from the creature in the room. It was answered immediately by distant howling coming from outside the house. The sounds made by these animals started to get closer and louder, until it seemed like they were right outside the bedroom window.

"Oh, Shit!" Declan's voice was lost in the thunderous baying.

The hall light came on, momentarily blinding the two clam thieves.

"What's going on here?" Sandi asked as he approached them from behind. "What have you done to Doreen?"

"We haven't done nothin, mister," Declan said.

"Sandi, help me." Doreen's voice was slurred and groggy.

Sandi continued forward, ready to push past them to enter the room.

"Wait, don't go in there," Declan tried to warn him. He stepped in front of Sandi to block his path, and before he could say anything more the creature appeared in the doorway. It snarled as it opened its mouth wide and bit down on his shoulder, making a loud crunching sound as bone and tissue was ground together. Declan yelled in agony as he was dragged inside. The beast growled savagely as it attacked Declan, whose efforts to defend himself with the knife he had in his possession were futile. He got in a few jabs and slashes, but he was no match for the power and ferocity of the Dog Man. Declan screamed as he was flayed open by claws and teeth. Blood spurted from severed arteries, covering the walls and pooling on the floor.

"Sandi," Doreen called, more sober and coherent.

Sandi brushed passed Brance, who stood staring in a near catatonic state as his friend was being ripped to pieces. Ignoring the carnage that was taking place in the room, Sandi walked inside and picked his helpless wife up off the bed. As he carried her out into the hallway, he grabbed Brance by the shirt collar with one hand and dragged him along down the hallway.

"Come on," he said.

Brance gave one last look back. Declan was no longer screaming. Only the wet sounds of warm innards being devoured. Body parts were torn off and scattered around the room like a bloody jigsaw puzzle,

Then came the most frightening sound of all, the shattering of glass as several more of the hybrid creatures burst through the window into the bedroom, whining loudly and ready to mate.

Chapter Nine

Sandi practically flung Brance into what he believed earlier was a storage room. When Sandi kicked the door shut, the lights automatically came on and he gently set his wife down on a leather couch. With a combination of astonishment and admiration, Brance watched Sandi attend to her, witnessing a side of the man that he did not expect. He had taken charge of a difficult and unforeseen situation, which was still ongoing, while looking out for someone he obviously cared deeply about, putting her wellbeing ahead of his own. Her nightgown was ripped and bloodied, and he covered her with a blanket and retrieved a first aid kit to dress her wounds.

Brance wandered around the room trying to get his bearings. He was drawn to the door, which had several locking mechanisms above the handle. He touched the wooden frame. It felt cold to the touch. When he knocked on it, he knew it was solid steel underneath the camouflage exterior. He moved over to the adjoining wall and wrapped on it. It had the same firmness, only with thick, steel-reinforced concrete underneath. He listened carefully, but he was unable to hear any of the chaos that was taking place in the adjacent bedroom.

It was some kind of safe room, Brance realized.

He turned to Sandi, whose only concern was for his wife. "Is she all right?" he asked.

Sandi set a pillow behind Doreen's head and gave her some pain medication and water.

"I'm better now," Doreen said, her voice faint and flat. "I couldn't move at all before, my arms, my legs. It was as if I was paralyzed. It was the strangest thing. And I don't remember what happened to me. Or how it happened." She raised the blanket involuntarily, holding it tightly under her chin.

Sandi shuttered at the thought of what Doreen was trying not to say. Earlier that night, he had experienced a similar feeling of immobility, which eventually wore off. "The important thing is you're ok," he told her. "Nothing can get in here."

"What kind of safe room is this anyway?" Brance asked. "I thought it was a spare room where you stored your junk."

"Yeah, well, I haven't gotten around to finishing it," Sandi said. "It doesn't have everything, but enough for us to get by for a while. It's fully ventilated. There's plenty of bottled water and non-perishable food. A generator for lighting, heating, and cooling. Some hand crank electrical appliances. There are closed-circuit cameras in every room, but no monitored alarm. We're on our own in here."

"Plumbing?" Brance submitted.

Sandi nodded toward the far corner of the room, where several plastic buckets were piled up. As Brance looked over, his attention was drawn to a digital safe with an electronic keypad that was built into the wall. He could only imagine the treasure trove of jewelry, cash and other bling that might be inside. Perhaps all was not lost, he thought. He still had his concealed knife, which Sandi didn't know about, and if he could wait it out in here with these people until it was safe to leave, he could still come out of this with a big score.

"Are the weapons locked up?" Brance asked. "You know, in case you need them."

Sandi considered his question with more than a little suspicion. "There's a taser and some pepper spray."

"No firearms?"

"I don't believe in guns."

Brance couldn't hold back a little smile.

"I didn't think I would need *any* of this," Sandi asserted. "The contractor talked me into it."

“Be glad he did.” Brance said.

Sandi leered at Brance, a fury he could no longer contain flaring up inside him. “What the hell are those things?” he fumed. “You know something.”

“Don’t look at me,” Brance responded. “I didn’t bring them here. The one that killed Declan was already here. It was…” He cleared his throat purposefully. “In bed with your wife.”

Sandi paused a moment to process the information, then looked at Doreen, their expressions mirror images of shock and terror.

“That was Delta?” She asked dubiously. It looked like she might throw up. “He’s a monster.”

“He’s not the only one,” Brance added. “There are others.”

“What do they want?” she asked.

“To continue the race,” Brance said. “To breed.”

Sandi looked at him sideways. “What are you talking about? I thought you didn’t know anything?”

“I admit,” Brance began, “to hear any kind of discussion about such a thing, it couldn’t be any more absurd. But I can tell you this, there are many Native American myths of creatures and spirits involving the revered animal, the dog. And an abundance of multi-cultural folklore about evil and murderous dogs, and of dogs breeding with humans."

"Who is this person, Sandi?" Doreen asked. "And why is he here?"

"You may as well tell her," Brance said with an air of mystery.

Sandi's eyes narrowed with contempt as they fixed on Brance.

"All right, I'll tell her," Brance began, pausing for dramatic effect. "My name is Brance Cultree. Your husband hired me to kill your dog. My associate and I were supposed to come by tomorrow, but we decided on tonight instead. And it looks like it was a good thing that we did. Though not for Declan, of course."

"Sandi, is he telling the truth?" Doreen asked.

Sandi averted his eyes.

Doreen's confused expression was replaced by alarm. "Did you know about these creatures?"

Sandi quickly turned and looked her in the eyes. "No, of course not," he shouted. "There was just something about that dog I didn't trust. It seemed like it wanted to get rid of me. Replace me. But I don't believe any of this fairy tale crap."

Doreen was satisfied with his response and turned her attention back to Brance.

"What was it you were saying about evil dogs?"

"These are far from fairy tales," Brance began, casting his eyes from Sandi to Doreen. "Just last year, a man in Australia claimed he was stalked by a bizarre half-dog, half-man creature in the outback. He was fishing in the bush when he heard something coming towards him from the woods. He said it let out a roar unlike anything he ever heard in his life."

Sandi scoffed. "Said the intoxicated Australian bushman."

"Reports of a half-human, half-dog creature first originated in Michigan in the 1800s and have since spread across the world. But long before this continent was settled by Europeans, Native Americans, including my people, have shared similar myths of terrifying hybrid dogs wandering the plains."

"Who are your people?" Doreen inquired.

"The Chinook, who are indigenous to the Pacific Northwest," he informed her. "Every culture has these stories. One of the most common is a Central American folk tale involving Cadejos, which are spirits that take on the likeness of dogs. White Cadejos are helpful spirits, but black Cadejos are malevolent. It is believed that there is one black Cadejo that is actually the embodiment of the Devil, which only comes out on nights when there is no visible moon and waits for unsuspecting humans to steal their souls. If you encounter a black Cadejo, your only hope is that a white one will show up to protect you. According to a Guatemala legend, one night a man was walking home and was accosted by robbers. Suddenly, a creature that he thought was a giant dog saved him, leaping on the robbers and tearing them to pieces. The man thought that the 'dog' was his friend and allowed the animal to accompany him home. Upon reaching the man's doorstep, however, the 'dog,' which was actually a black Cadejo, fell upon him and ripped him apart."

"What about the breeding part you mentioned," Doreen interjected, raising her upper body off the couch and leaning forward attentively. "Tell us about that."

Sandi let out an exasperated breath but held his tongue.

"There is an ancient story about a village girl who lived with her father and refused to marry any of the villagers that her father selected for her. She told her father that she'd rather marry a dog, and eventually she did just that. She and her dog-husband went on to have ten children, five of which were perfectly ordinary dogs, but the other five were a blend of man and animal.

"Then one day, the girl's father grew tired of feeding the entire litter and devised a plan to get rid of his grand-beasts. He moved his daughter, her dog-husband, and their litter to a deserted island, telling the dog-husband that each day he would leave bags of meat for the dog-family on the shore, forcing the dog-man to retrieve the food by swimming across the body of water.

"One morning, instead of meat, the girl's father filled the bags with rocks. The dog-man, unable to swim with the heavy bags, drowned trying to take what he thought was food to his family. The girl was beside herself with grief, for she had come to love her dog-husband. In an act of vengeance, she ordered her dog-children to swim ashore and chew off her father's feet and hands. Afterward, she was unable to bear the resemblance that her dog-children had to her beloved dog-husband, so she sent all of them into the wilderness to fend for themselves. The dog-men are purported to still be out there, hungry, with a taste for human flesh."

"So, what exactly are you saying?" Sandi demanded.

"Simple," Brance stated. "Your wife must have a lineage with the original bloodline of the creatures that have invaded your home, and they have sought her out so that they can repopulate the species."

"This is such horse shit," Sandi fumed.

"Wait a minute, Sandi" Doreen began. "If you think about it, there are similarities between these stories and the things that we've both experienced. Like the guy who befriended the dog and then was attacked when he took the animal into his home."

Sandi glared at her in disbelief. "You seriously can't believe any of this?" he beseeched her. "Tell me you don't."

"I don't know what to believe," Doreen said. Feeling strong enough, she got up off the couch and made her way over to Sandi with the blanket still wrapped around her. "Something beyond our comprehension is going on here, Sandi. Maybe he can shed some light on this."

Brance grinned and walked over to the small desk that held a computer, among other electronic devices. "Does this thing work?"

Sandi didn't say anything but joined Brance at the terminal. A few clicks of the button and the screen displayed every room in the house. The individual squares were tinted green from the night vision cameras that illuminated the dark rooms. The images were static in every box except for one.

"Bring up that one," Brance said, pointing to the one labeled MASTER BEDROOM.

A moment later the screen was filled with frenetic motion.

"What the –" Sandi stared in disbelief at what he was witnessing.

There were five creatures in the room, though four were considerably smaller than the largest one. Their human anatomy extended only up to their necks, their heads and faces a grotesque fusion of man and canine. This hybrid breed had the ability to turn almost entirely into men - all but their heads at least - when excited and engaged in the act of mating with human females who shared their bloodline. This shapeshifting was not known to many, and was not part of the legends because it had not always existed, but rather something that had evolved over time as a survival advantage. It was the same process that allowed them to develop a form of mind control, the kind of which lured both Sandi and Doreen into a hypnotic dream state.

This was the first time that any of them had been able to revert to their human forms, and they were not about to let the opportunity go to waste. They were tearing the room apart, urinating everywhere, pleasuring themselves, humping the furniture and each other. It was a riot of hormones, a vulgar, chaotic orgy.

As disturbing as these images were, neither Sandi nor Doreen could look away from the computer screen. Brance was no expert on the supernatural, but because of his heritage, it was easier for him to accept things that could not be explained.

Suddenly the beasts began to leave the room in search of Doreen. It was almost as if they had just realized that she wasn't in there with them. Her scent did not extend very far outside the bedroom, however, and they stopped in the hallway directly outside of the safe room. Even through the dense concrete that fortified all four walls and the ceiling, they had been able to track her. They began throwing themselves up against the steel door, scratching and clawing and screeching in frustration as their efforts failed to get them any closer to their prize.

Dog Man approached slowly, walking more upright than the others, all of whom scrambled to get out of his way, fear residing in their eyes. Dog Man paused and looked directly up at the small camera embedded in the ceiling above the door. His pug face, jowly cheeks and menacing red eyes, indeed, lent him the look of the devil. The mutant animal seemed to comprehend its plight, staring up with a sense of affirmation, projecting a kind of dignity and refinement, and carrying itself more like a human than any of the others in the pack.

Suddenly, Dog Man raised one leg and peed on the floor. A puddle of urine seeped under the bottom of the door into the safe room.

"Look," Brance said, drawing Sandi's attention back on the computer screen, where a red light flickered. When Sandi hit a button on the keypad, the screen split in half, displaying a second image from a camera in the foyer. There was movement outside the front door, and then all at once it practically busted off its hinges, opening inward and followed by two sturdy figures.

"There's more of them." Sandi said.

"Uh-uh," Brance corrected him. "They're carrying guns." He knew exactly who they were, and he knew he was in trouble.

Then a half dozen more men, all armed to the teeth, followed the other two inside.

Now they were all in trouble.

Chapter Ten

Alberto thought they were prepared for anything. He had learned from a contractor who did business with the cartel that the homeowner had a safe room in the house, and he expected that the family would have already retreated to the bunker by the time he and Hector could reach them. If they hadn't, this raid would be over in a matter of minutes. And even if they were locked down behind concrete walls and a steel door, getting to them wouldn't be a problem. When Alberto informed Edgar Omar Fuentes, aka El Ratone, about the safe room, the crew boss knew just what was needed, having his men bring enough plastic explosives to bust Fort Knox sky high. They were also packing M82- semi-automatic rifles, which could penetrate concrete walls, as well as a M72 shoulder-fired rocket launcher thrown in for good measure

With the combined firepower they were bringing, Alberto figured they would be in an out of there before the smoke cleared.

Alberto and Hector, each carrying AK-47s, lead the assault, moving methodically along the ground floor, checking each room as they made their way down the hallway to the kitchen. Finding no one, they doubled back, meeting the six assault-rifle-carrying assassins, including El Ratone, in the foyer near the front of the stairs. Alberto directed the hired guns to head upstairs while he and Hector started down the hallway on the opposite end of the house. They didn't get very far before they caught sight of feverish dancing movements in the deep shadows. The dancers were not defined, but their eyes were somehow glowing even in the near complete darkness. Alberto and Hector stopped and raised their weapons, not sure what they were seeing until Alberto flicked the light switch that was right beside him.

"What the fuck!" Hector screeched as the hallway was illuminated with soft light from the rows of wall sconces. Then he started laughing at the absurdity of five naked jitterbugging dudes. They had long hair covering most of their bodies, though not nearly long enough as far as Hector was concerned. They were sporting stiff erections. "What the hell are these people into?"

The dog men halted at once and gazed back at the hit men. Four of them seemed to consider the men warily. The eyes of one of them, who was much larger than the other four - in every way – continued to radiate a laser-like luminescence. This one was clearly the leader, standing tall, unintimidated. The others appeared to be waiting for an order to follow. Both men instinctively trained their guns on Dog Man, which was what he wanted.

It was just a low growl, but the dog men heard their leaders' command and they swiftly reacted, running headlong toward the men with the long guns. Dog Man sprang out of the line of fire just as the shots began to ring out.

The explosive gunfire alerted El Ratone and his men that the assault was underway, and they immediately headed downstairs to lend their assistance.

When Alberto and Hector emptied their 30-round magazines, they quickly reloaded and looked around for something to aim at. But the lot of them had vanished, and on the ground was a dead dog.

"Where'd they go?" Hector asked.

There were rooms on either side of the hall, the doors standing open. Only one door was closed. Alberto put his hand on the false wood and pressed his palm against the surface, feeling the cold, firm steel underneath. Then he poked a finger into one of the bullet holes in the wall. Beneath the plaster, he could feel the rough texture of the concrete.

The thunderous charging of feet from the other end of the hallway prompted Alberto and Hector to raise their reloaded rifles in that direction. When El Ratone and his men rounded the corner, they all stopped and did the same, training their guns on each other.

"Hold it, hold it," Alberto shouted, raising his AK to the ceiling. "Did you guys see any of them?"

"Who?" El Ratone asked.

There was a moment's hesitation before Hector spoke out. "About a half dozen ugly naked dudes."

"Say again."

"Have your guys check all these rooms," Alberto told El Ratone "And that is the door we need to blast." He nodded at the closed door at the end of the hall.

El Ratone gave the order to his men and then set about applying a malleable light brown substance to the door while Alberto went over to inspect the remains of the dog that seemed to have been killed in the crossfire. It had been struck multiple times. Its chest had been torn open and its innards were spilling out.

"Where'd that thing come from?" Hector asked beside him. "I didn't see any dog with them."

Alberto poked the tip of his rifle into the flesh and guts of the animal, moving them around as if he was in search of something.

"What are you looking for?" Hector had to know.

"Strange," was all he said in response.

"I'd say so," Hector said with a chuckle.

Alberto looked at him without expression.

"It's ready," El Ratone said when the detonator was set. He'd molded the C4 so as to direct the blast inward, applying more than enough to blow the door and breach the safe room.

"All right, stand back," Alberto warned, and then nodded to El Ratone when everyone had slipped into a room, putting as many walls as possible between them and the explosives.

When the detonator switch was hit, all hell broke loose, just as Dog Man had planned.

As soon as the men had entered the house, Dog Man picked up the Almond smell of the explosive material. The only chance the pack had was to attack the men at the most vulnerable moment, which would be in the immediate aftermath of the explosion, when there was a lot of confusion and smoke.

The violent shock wave rocked the entire house, producing a deafening sound and more than enough energy to pop the steel door open like a can of tuna fish.

As soon as the hit men came out of cover, the dog men struck. They were back in dog form now, on all fours, and working together as a bloodthirsty pack. They moved faster and with more precision than anything any of them had ever seen in any breed of dog. The men didn't know what hit them as they were ambushed by the animals, who sank their teeth into their flesh, inflicting them with crippling wounds.

The canines retreated before the men could get off a defensive shot. Dazed and bloodied by the bite-and-run attack, the men held a tight line, their backs against the same wall of the hallway.

"What the *fuck* is going on here?" Hector screamed, holding the gaping wound in his thigh closed with one hand while gripping the AK-47 in the other.

"That's why I'd like to know," El Ratone said. "What have you got my men into? Let's go get those motherfuckers. Jesus, you and Harold check the rooms on this side of the hall. Amado, Arturo, Miguel, take the other."

"No, wait, that's just what they want," Alberto objected, but it was too late. The men had already been dispatched.

Alberto understood this strategy well. A skillful predator will pursue animals that are bigger and stronger by repeatedly attacking and backing off. When the prey is sufficiently injured and tired, that's when they go in for the kill. They try to separate the stronger animals, getting each one alone, and then pick them off one at a time as a pack. It was a survival tactic that has stood the test of time in the animal kingdom.

Now it was man against beast.

The animals were all in the room that Arturo had gone into, and his screams rang out for all to hear as he was being savaged by the four remaining dogs. Amado was the first one to respond to his associate's distress, and he charged recklessly into the room, gun blazing. The rounds from the semi-automatic weapon produced a flickering light show, like an electrical storm, in the room. There were squeals and screams, and when it was over, two men were dead and four dogs raced out of the kill zone, though one was limping, dragging a hind leg that had taken a bullet.

The gangsters in the hallway all fired at the animals, but they missed their fast-moving targets. The shots echoed down the hallway as the dogs bounded into the room where Miguel was waiting for them. He didn't fare any better, however, though he did manage to take out the injured beta-omega, who could not maintain the speed and agility needed to evade the assassin's bullets.

The three strongest dogs in the pack were in a blood frenzy as they sought out Harold and Jesus, who they could sense were the weakest in the human pack. The two men were hiding behind a standing mirror in one of the rooms, but the animals could smell them, and they silently stalked them. The killers were about to be killed, and just as their own victims would often experience before being assassinated, Harold and Jesus did not hear death approach until it was upon them.

While all this was going on, Alberto, Hector and El Ratone made their way into the safe room, where dust from the explosion was still settling. Debris was strewn all over the floor. Parts of the walls and ceiling around the door were completely destroyed, exposing the concrete shell beneath the sheet rock and acoustic tiles above. The assassins swept through the wreckage. The room wasn't very big, and it didn't take long to determine that there was no one there. Alberto, however, remained watchful. He was looking for a trap door handle or knob, and he soon spotted it, a barn door type pull plate, which was the same color as the wall. He signaled to the other men, pointing to the spot and holding his rifle in front of him. He approached slowly, then swiftly reached for the handle and rolled the heavy steel door open as he directed the barrel of his AK-47 at the three people huddled inside. It was just a regular closet, but it was insulated for extra protection.

"Out," Alberto ordered the three captives.

Sandi and Doreen exited together first. Brance reluctantly followed.

"That's far enough," Alberto said. They all stopped instantly. He looked Sandi in the eye. "You, open that safe over there." Turning to Brance, he said, "You, say your prayers."

"Wait." Brance held his hands out in front of him defensively. "You can't do this."

"I'm not," Alberto said. "Hector, kill this piece of shit."

"Gladly," Hector said as he approached.

El Ratone stepped forward. “After what happened to my men, let me do it.”

“Why don’t you both do it,” Alberto suggested.

The two assassins looked at one another and nodded their consent, then raised their assault rifles simultaneously.

Brance could only close his eyes and brace for the inevitable, hoping the end would come quickly and with little or no pain.

Not a moment after he had this thought, he heard two loud pops. He was thankful that he didn’t feel anything, but he knew something wasn’t right. The sounds had not been made by AK-47s, and they came from behind him. When he opened his eyes, he saw the two men standing perfectly still, their jaws slack and mouths open slightly. Their eyes expressed shock as blood trickled down the sides of their head from small caliber bullet holes in their temples. All at once they slumped to the floor, dead.

Brance looked around, and to his utter amazement he saw Sandi in a “boxer-type” shooting stance with a 9mm Glock 17 in his hand. The wall safe that was open beside him contained only a couple boxes of ammo.

“Get down, Doreen,” yelled Sandi, expecting return gunfire from Alberto, who was standing behind his wife. Brance hit the deck as gunfire erupted. As a moving target, Sandi was more difficult to hit. In the volley of gunshots, however, he was struck in the right calf. It tore through the muscle, obliterating it and he went down hard, losing his gun and striking his head on the exposed concrete.

Everyone in the room was so preoccupied with shooting or avoiding getting shot that they didn't notice the three animals that had entered and were all around them, their muzzles soaked with blood.

When Alberto went to replace his empty magazine with a fresh one, two of the dogs pounced on him while Dog Man leapt on Doreen. Alberto was big and powerful, and taking him down would not have been an easy task under any circumstance, even for these two young animals. They attacked him aggressively, ripping and tearing his clothes, but they could not hurt him. He was wearing full tactical body armor that protected the most vulnerable areas, including his chest, abdomen, groin, and upper and lower extremities, where the largest arteries were located. Alberto was able to fend off the canines as he continued trying to lock the new clip into his rifle. Teeth tore flesh from his forearms, but they were unable to mortally wound the last gangster. Finally, he was able to insert the magazine. As he got to his feet, he came up firing. The dogs' growls turned to yelps, and as they took multiple rounds from the high-powered weapons, their bodies practically liquified.

Doreen looked around for Sandi, and when she saw his prone body, unmoving, lying in a pool of blood, she called his name and rushed over to him. Nearby, Alberto collected himself and walked slowly over to where Brance was lying on the ground. Suddenly, Dog Man jumped out of the shadows and clamped its teeth into Alberto's neck, just above the collar of his body armor. A large portion of his jugular was shielded, but the powerful jaws and sharp teeth destroyed tissue and crunched into the vertebrae of his cervical spine, instantly paralyzing Alberto, who went down in a heap. Dog Man continue digging into the man's neck, managing to completely sever the spinal cord, and he still wasn't satisfied. It seemed as if he wanted to take the head for a prize, and he almost accomplished it, managing to turn the Alberto's head all the way around so that his chin was resting on his back.

Dog Man lifted its head, gore dripping from both sides of its mouth, and looked over to where Doreen was sitting with Sandi's head resting in her lap. The beast growled and rose up on all fours, padding over to the couple as Doreen squirmed helplessly.

Brance saw that Sandi's gun was out of reach, and even if he went for it, he had no chance of getting it before the creature got to him.

Dog Man eased his nose in close to Sandi's face, smelling his next victim. Sandi wasn't dead, only incapacitated, but the hybrid creature still believed that this man posed the biggest threat to what needed to be accomplished with Doreen. That instinct proved fatal when Brance suddenly rose up, Bowie knife in hand, and buried the blade into Dog Man's side, piercing its chest and striking the animal's knot-like heart. The beast bellowed as Brance levered the knife back and forth in order to achieve maximum tissue damage, and then quickly removed the blade, ensuring rapid blood loss and near instant death.

Epilogue

Sandi's gunshot injury, although disfiguring, was not life-threating. There was no damage to the bones of his lower leg, but the calf muscle was completely destroyed. Once out of the rehabilitation hospital, he was able to walk with the assistance of a cane, something he would need for the rest of his life. What had the potential to be more grievous was the brain trauma that he suffered. When he fell, his head struck the concrete wall with enough force to fracture his skull. While no significant harm was done to the underlying brain tissue, the swelling resulted in permanent memory loss. He subsequently had no recollection of anything that happened the night of the massacre in the Denny-Blaine estate. Even after reading about it and watching stories in the news, it did not seem real. It was easy for him to put the whole incident behind him, which was a blessing. An even greater blessing was learning that Doreen was pregnant with twins, a boy and girl. It was the fulfillment of a dream for the couple, and it was just what was needed to make them both whole again.

They moved out of Seattle, and away from the Pacific Northwest altogether. They relocated about as far from Seattle as they could, settling outside Washington, D.C. to raise their family.

Brance was sent to a correctional facility north of Seattle as authorities tried to determine what his exact role was in all the bloodshed. However, he was not there very long before he escaped, or more accurately, disappeared. It was on the second day of his detention in state prison that he went missing. Numerous inmates reporting seeing Brance in the rec yard that afternoon, but he never reported back to his cell, and he was never found. It was a complete mystery what happened to him, and it's unknown if he successfully escaped, or possibly met some other end.

Onc other anomaly that could not be explained was how a dog found its way into the prison yard that day. It was a large mixed breed with white fluffy fur and pale blue eyes. No one came forward to claim ownership of the animal, so one of the guards set it loose outside the front gates. The dog happily scampered off into the open field behind the Monroe Correctional Complex and into the neighborhood beyond.

As for Dog Man, his demise was not in vain. Its bloodline was not broken. Not only had it survived, but with an added infusion of human DNA, the hybrid race would one day grow powerful and thrive once again.

About Paul Lonardo

I am a freelance writer and I have authored numerous titles over the past two decades, both fiction and nonfiction books in a variety of genres. Most recently, "The Legend of Lake Incunabula," a collection of dark fantasy stories, was released in March 2022. I am a member of HWA.

I studied filmmaking/screenwriting at Columbia College - Hollywood. I earned an A.S. from Mount Ida College and a B.A. in English from the University of Rhode Island. I live in Lincoln, RI with my wife and son.

Social Media

Twitter: @PaulLonardo
Website: https://www.thegoblinpitcher.com/
Goodreads:
https://www.goodreads.com/author/show/734960.Paul_Lonardo

LibraryThing:
https://www.librarything.com/profile/PaulLonardo
AuthorsDen: https://www.authorsden.com/visit/author.asp?authorid=178242
LinkedIn:
https://www.linkedin.com/in/paul-lonardo-b88b4b12/
BookBub: https://www.bookbub.com/profile/paul-lonardo
Alignable:
https://www.alignable.com/lincoln-ri/paul-lonardo-palonardo-aol-com-author-ghostwriter
Horror Writers Association:
http://hwa46.wildapricot.org/page-1683781
Association of Rhode Island Authors:
https://www.riauthors.org/authors/
The Author's Guild:
https://go.authorsguild.org/members/5657
Barnes & Noble:
https://www.barnesandnoble.com/s/paul%20lonardo/_/N-8q8
Amazon: https://www.amazon.com/Paul Lonardo/e/B000APQ0Z4/ref=dp_byline_cont_pop_ebooks_1

Made in the USA
Middletown, DE
03 September 2022

71982148R00062